t of Dysart

W

KIDNAPPED

ROBERT LOUIS STEVENSON
illustrated by N. C. WYETH

A SCRIBNER STORYBOOK CLASSIC
Atheneum Books for Young Readers
New York London Toronto Sydney

Atheneum Books for Young Readers

An imprint of Simon & Schuster Children's Publishing Division

1230 Avenue of the Americas

New York, New York 10020

Book designed by Abelardo Martínez

The text for this book is set in Palatino.

The illustrations for this book are rendered in oil paints.

Manufactured in China

First Edition

2 4 6 8 10 9 7 5 3 1

Library of Congress Cataloging-in-Publication Data

Stevenson, Robert Louis, 1850-1894.

Kidnapped / Robert Louis Stevenson ; illustrated by N. C. Wyeth.—1st ed.

p.   cm. — (A Scribner storybook classic)

Abridgment copyright by Timothy Meis.

Summary: A sixteen-year-old orphan is kidnapped by his villainous uncle, but later escapes and becomes involved in the struggle of the Scottish highlanders against English rule.

ISBN 0-689-86542-2

1. Scotland—History—18th century—Juvenile fiction. [1. Scotland—History—18th century—Fiction.
2. Adventure and adventurers—Fiction.] I. Wyeth, N. C. (Newell Convers), 1882-1945, ill.
II. Meis, Timothy. III. Title. IV. Series.

PZ7 .S8482Ki   2004

[Fic]—dc22   2003016812

PROLOGUE

*T*he Highlands of Scotland in the north of that country are dotted with lonesome moors, rocky crags on granite braes, vast stretches of windblown heather, and storm-filled rills that flow down the mountainsides and empty into lochs of icy cold water. The harsh yet beautiful landscape is reflected in the character of the people of that area: fiercely independent, proud, quarrelsome, and loyal to a fault. As Scotsmen, they prize their independence and are always willing to fight for it. And so in the seventeenth century when England replaced King James II, the man whom the Highlanders considered their rightful king, with William of Orange, a Protestant (because they feared the Catholic James would be more loyal to the pope than to Englishmen), these proud Scots readied their weapons; for they dreamed of the day when they would lead a rebellion to restore the real heir to the throne.

And in 1745, James II's grandson, Prince Charles Edward, sailed from France to Scotland, determined to lead a rebellion that would put him on the English throne. Numerous clans and individual Scotsmen (who were called Jacobites from the Latin *Jacobus,* meaning "James") took up the cause and rallied behind Charles Edward, whom they called Bonnie Prince Charlie.

Although many Highland clans supported the prince, not enough did to enable him to raise an army large enough to threaten the British throne. And so on the sixteenth of April in 1746 his military force was defeated in the Battle of Culloden at Drummossie Moor near Inverness, Scotland.

But still there were those who refused to give up the dream.

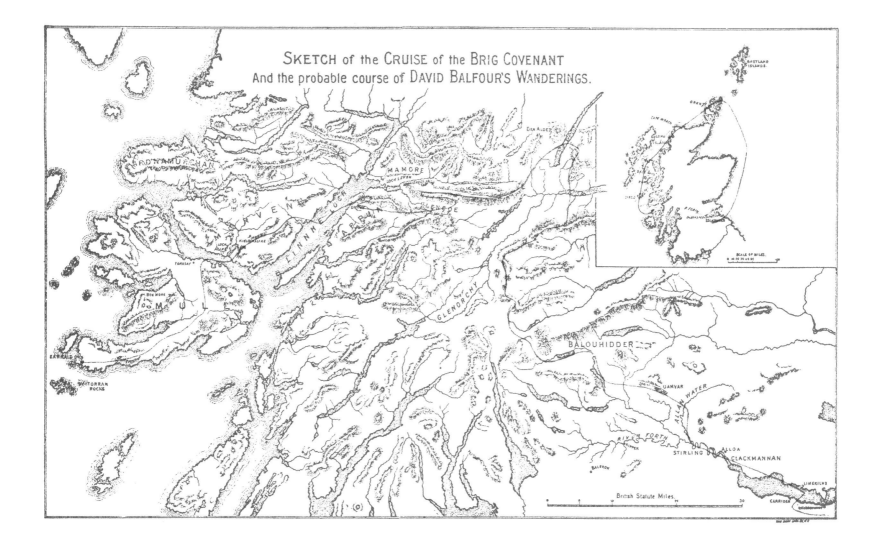

SKETCH of the CRUISE of the BRIG COVENANT
And the probable course of DAVID BALFOUR'S WANDERINGS.

I will begin the story of my adventures early in the month of June, the year of grace 1751, on the morning when I took the key out of the door of my late father's house for the last time. Mr. Campbell, the minister of Essendean, was waiting for me by the garden gate.

"Tell me, Davie," he said with a wistful smile, "are ye sorry to leave Essendean?"

"Yes and no, Mr. Campbell. I have been very happy in Essendean, but I wish to see more of the world than this small village. The only things that remain for me here are the graves of my parents."

"Yes, lad, about that," Mr. Campbell said with a certain heaviness. "Your father gave me charge of your inheritance. 'When I am gone,' he said, 'give my boy this letter of introduction and start him off to the House of Shaws, not far from Cramond. That is the place I came from.'"

"The House of Shaws, what is that?" I asked.

"Don't ye know, Davie?" he asked. "That is the name you bear—David Balfour of Shaws. I have heard stories from people passing through this village of a great mansion near Cramond known as the House of Shaws." He then gave me the letter, which was addressed: *To Ebenezer Balfour, Esquire, of Shaws.*

My heart was beating hard at this great prospect now suddenly opening before me. I had relatives—relatives who might be able to help me start in the world!

"A lad like you should get to Cramond in two days' walk. It's not far from Edinburgh," Mr. Campbell continued. "I hope that ye shall be well received by your relations at the House of Shaws."

With that he prayed aloud for a little while and then suddenly embraced me.

After he gave me a little money, he whipped about, and crying good-bye, set off by the way he had come.

I was sorrowful at the departure but also overjoyed to get out of that quiet countryside and go to a great, busy house, among rich and respected gentlefolk of my own name and blood.

On the afternoon of the second day, coming to the top of a hill, I saw Edinburgh, the grandest city in Scotland, smoking like a kiln before me. There was a flag upon the castle, and ships moving in the water. The glorious sight caused my country heart to leap into my mouth. As a boy, I had always dreamed of seeing that great city, but my father rarely left Essendean, and so I never had the opportunity. I hoped that my adventures would someday lead there, but first I was eager to find my relations in the town nearby.

A passing shepherd gave me directions to the village of Cramond. A little farther on, I began to inquire of the House of Shaws. It was a word that seemed to surprise those I asked. I began to take it into my head that there was something peculiar about the Shaws.

I came upon an old woman, stooped and wearing a ratty shawl, and asked if she had ever heard of my destination. The woman's face lit up with a malignant anger. "The House of Shaws!" she cried. "I spit upon the ground and crack my thumb at it."

I took this expression to mean that she placed a curse upon the house. I thought this strange, but wondered even more what she thought of Mr. Balfour of the Shaws.

"He is no kind of man at all," she said. "It's none of my affair, but if you'll take a word from me, you'll keep clear of the Shaws." Still, she pointed out the house, and before I could ask her anything more, she hurried off down the road. I looked where she had pointed and I saw, to my dismay, a house that

"Are ye sorry to leave Essendean?"

once was probably a grand, respectable mansion. But now it appeared to be in a sorry state of disrepair. No road led up to it, no smoke arose from any of the chimneys, and there was no garden to be seen. My heart sank.

I sat down for a long while and stared at the House of Shaws. At last the sun went down, and I saw a pitiful scroll of smoke climb lazily from the chimney. I decided that as I had come so far already I was bound out of mere self-respect to meet my uncle.

I got up and walked toward the house. The nearer I got to it, the drearier it appeared. One wing of the house appeared never to have been finished. The upper floors' uncompleted steps and stairs jutted into the sky. Bats flew in and out of the windows. Was this the palace I thought I was coming to?

I approached cautiously, and heard someone rattling dishes, and a little dry cough that came in fits, but there was no sound of speech. I lifted my hand with a faint heart and knocked once. Then I stood and waited. A whole minute passed away, and nothing stirred but the bats overhead. I knocked again, and again there was no sound but the ticking clock inside.

I was of two minds as to run away or not, but it began to rain, and rain hard. I gave the door a kick, and shouted out for Mr. Balfour. Then I heard the cough right overhead. I jumped back and looked up to behold a man's head in a white nightcap, and the barrel of a gun at one of the windows.

"It's loaded," said a voice.

CHAPTER TWO

"I have come here with a letter of introduction," I said as the rain began to fully soak my clothes, "to Mr. Ebenezer Balfour of Shaws. Is he at home?"

"Who are ye?" asked the man with the gun.

"I am David Balfour."

After quite a long pause, and a curious change of voice, he asked, "Is your father dead?"

I was so surprised at this question that I could find no voice to answer, but stood staring.

"Ay," the man resumed, "he's dead, no doubt. Otherwise, why would you be here?" He was quiet for a moment, and then he asked more forcefully, "And your mother?"

"Four years now," I replied, finding my tongue.

"Ay," his voice softened a bit. "She was a bonnie lass."

And then there was a pause in which neither of us spoke.

"Well," he said at length, "I'll let ye in." And he disappeared from the window. Presently there came a great rattling of chains and bolts, and the door was cautiously opened.

"Go into the kitchen and touch nothing," he said brusquely. In the near dark I groped my way forward and entered the kitchen. In the dim hearth fire I beheld the most dismal room I think I ever put my eyes on. Besides a bowl of porridge, a horn spoon, and a small cup on the table, there was not another thing in that great, stone-vaulted, empty chamber but two chests along the wall and a cupboard with some old books upon it.

As soon as the man rebolted the door he joined me. In appearance he was a stooping, narrow-shouldered, clay-faced creature, and his age might have been anything between fifty and seventy. He hadn't shaved in some time, but what distressed me most was that he would neither take his eyes away nor look me squarely in the face.

"Let's see the letter," he said.

I told him the letter was for Mr. Balfour, not for him.

"And who do you think I am?" said he. "Give me Alexander's letter!"

"You know my father's name?"

"It would be strange if I didn't know my own brother's name," he said sharply.

My father's brother! My father had never spoken of a brother. And yet, all I felt was a tremendous disappointment. I handed him the letter. Stooping over the fire, he turned the letter over and over in his hands.

"What brought you here?" he asked, cunningly. "Money?"

"I was told that I had kinsfolk and indulged the hope that they might help me out in life." And then, rather rashly, I stood and declared, "But I am no beggar. I look for no favors that are not freely given."

My uncle sat down to his porridge and his expression gave no indication of his mood. All that was heard between us were the keys in his hand that jingled with each spasm of his nervous twitch. The silence made me even more irritable.

"Do you think I am a country Johnny with no learning?" I asked as I grabbed a book of Latin from the open cupboard. I blew away the dust and had every intention of reading from it aloud when I saw the inscription on the front page. On the flyleaf, plainly written in my father's hand, was: TO MY BROTHER EBENEZER ON HIS FIFTH BIRTHDAY. Instantly a question came into my head: "Tell me, who between you two was the eldest?" I asked.

He jumped upon his stool, dropping his spoon. "Why do ye ask me that?" he said as he caught me by the breast of my jacket. This time he looked straight into my eyes. His own were little and almost drained of color, but nervous like a bird's, always blinking and winking strangely.

All that was heard between us were the keys in his hand that jingled with each spasm of his nervous twitch.

"Take your hand from my jacket," I protested, pushing him away. "This is no way to behave." I began to think my uncle was perhaps insane and might be dangerous. On the other hand, there came into my mind a story of a poor lad who was a rightful heir whose wicked kinsman tried to keep him from his own house. If this were the case with Ebenezer, it would explain why he was treating me so ghastly.

I now began to imitate his covert looks, so that we stood like a cat and mouse, each stealthily observing the other.

"David," he said finally. "I've been thinking. Since you are my brother's boy, I should give you an allowance. No doubt Alexander would have approved."

I was struck dumb by his sudden generosity and struggled to thank him.

"Not a word!" he said. "No thanks . . . but," he continued, "I am growing old and would appreciate some help around the house and the garden."

I reflected upon the fact that we were blood relatives and that meant something to me. I expressed my readiness to serve.

"Grand," he said. "I keep all my money in a chest in the tower at the far end of the house." He gave me a rusty key. "You can only get into it from the outside, for that part of the house is not finished. Go up the stairs, and you'll find the chest at the top. Fetch it and I shall pay you."

"Can I have a light to see, sir?" I asked.

"Alas," he replied. "I'm nearly out of candles."

"Very well, sir," I said. "Are the stairs good?"

"Ay, they're grand," he said, and then he added as I was leaving, "Keep to the wall; there's no banister. But the stairs are grand underfoot."

Out I went into the night. While the rain had stopped, the wind was moaning in the distance and the sky was even blacker than before. Feeling along the wall, I soon came to the stair-tower door at the far end of the unfinished wing. I put the key into the keyhole and had just turned it when a thunderclap awoke the night. The whole sky lit up with wild fire and went black again. In the sudden flash of light, I looked up to see the tower standing menacingly over me, some five stories high.

I stepped into the tower and, minding my uncle's words about the banisters, kept close to the tower side, feeling my way up and up in the pitch darkness. Again the summer lightning came and went. This time I cried out—the passing brightness showed me that if I had taken one more step, I would have stepped where there was no stone and fallen to my death, for the stairs went no higher.

The thought came quick to me: My uncle had sent me up here to die!

I got down upon my hands and knees, and as slowly as a snail, feeling before me every inch, I began to descend the stairs. When I reached the ground level, I put my head out and looked toward the kitchen. The door, which was shut behind me when I left, now stood open. No doubt my uncle was waiting to hear my death scream.

I stepped silently into the room, came close behind my uncle where he sat, and, clapping my two hands down upon his shoulders, shouted, "Ah-ha!"

My uncle gave a kind of broken cry like a sheep's bleat, flung up his arms, and tumbled to the floor. He had fainted dead away!

CHAPTER THREE

*T*he next morning I unlocked the door to the room I had placed my uncle in. I grabbed him from his bed and demanded he tell me the real reason he sent me up the stair tower.

"A bit of jest," he croaked uneasily.

"You lie!" I said. "I can guess that there is no chest at the top of the tower."

"I lied, I lied," my uncle spat out quickly between coughs. "Your unexpected arrival put me in a bit of a panic. Can you forgive me?"

"I will if you make good my situation. There is something amiss in the relationship between my father and you." I recalled how he had avoided answering my question over who was the older of the two.

"I will take you to Queensferry this very day," he interrupted. "I have business with a sea captain. While we are there, we can see a lawyer, Mr. Rankeillor. He will explain to you about your father and all that you have coming to you."

Satisfied, I released him to dress in proper clothes. And before the clock struck eight, we set out for the nearby port town.

Our journey was spent in silence, for neither of us spoke to each other, nor did anyone passing by say anything to my uncle Ebenezer. As we walked along a river, the Firth of Forth, just east of Queensferry, I saw dozens of ships bobbing in the tide.

"There's the *Covenant*." My uncle pointed with his crooked index finger. "I am to see the captain of that ship regarding an investment."

I gazed out upon the *Covenant*. There appeared to be a seagoing bustle on board; yards were swinging into place, and as the wind blew from that quarter, I could hear the song of the sailors as they pulled upon the ropes. Yet, after

I had listened, I looked at that ship with an extreme abhorrence for there was something unholy about it, though I knew not what.

I wondered if this ship, or any of the ships in the harbor, was involved with the Scottish rebels, the Jacobites who were rife in this part of the country. It was well known that some of the rebels, who thought that a Scotsman should sit on the throne of England, would hire boats to take them to France, where many other rebels lived in exile. The only other thing that I knew about these Jacobites was that they were being routed out of their homes by a British agent named Colin Roy Campbell, nicknamed the Red Fox.

I had never seen a Jacobite, but as a lowland lad I was taught that these rebels were wrong and cowardly and that I should love our country's protector, King George II of England.

My thoughts were filled with ships full of rebels evading British patrols, of fighting and dying and hiding from the law. But these daydreams evaporated as soon as we came to our destination, the inn at Queensferry, where I met Captain Hoseason, captain of the *Covenant.* He was a tall, dark, sober-looking man who, in spite of the heat of the room, wore a thick sea-jacket, buttoned to the neck, and a tall hairy cap drawn down over his ears. Yet I never saw any man look cooler and more self-possessed than he.

"I am proud to see you, Mr. Balfour," he said in a fine deep voice when we were introduced. I returned the compliment and sat, but soon grew uncomfortable in that room with my uncle. And though I had made a promise to myself not to let my kinsman out of sight, I was both so impatient for a nearer look at the sea, and so sickened by the closeness of the room, that when my uncle suggested I could "run downstairs and play awhile," I was fool enough to take him at his word.

Away I went, leaving the two men to a bottle and a great mass of papers. I crossed the road and walked down upon the beach. In the distance I saw the

Covenant beginning to shake out her sails. I looked, too, at the seamen in the skiff at the wharf—big brown fellows, some in shirts, some with jackets, one with a brace of pistols stuck into his pockets, and all with their case knives. I did not linger long.

The first properly dressed gentleman I encountered I stopped and asked if he knew the whereabouts of a lawyer by the name of Mr. Rankeillor. The man seemed as if he was about to answer when he looked me straight in the face for several moments as though he recognized something about me.

"Are you a Balfour?" he asked.

"Son of Alexander," I said proudly.

"Ay." He smiled. "There's no doubt there. I've not seen him for many years, but you are the spitting image of him, not that wretched Ebenezer."

"You know them! Tell me," I asked hurriedly, "who was the eldest?"

"Alexander, of course," he exclaimed. Upon seeing my astonishment, he continued, "So you won't know the answer to the riddle either."

"What riddle?" I asked.

"Well, by custom and by law, a family's fortune always passes to the eldest son. Everyone expected the House of Shaws to go to Alexander after their father, your grandfather, died. How it came to be in Ebenezer's possession is a riddle to many of us in town."

With that revelation, I lost the strength in my legs and rested upon the cobblestone curb. If the house should have passed to my father, then by rights it would now be mine. How long I sat dazed, I know not, but when I looked up, instead of seeing the man with whom I had recently conversed, I saw instead the broad shoulders and wide grin of Captain Hoseason looking down upon me.

He heaved me up with his strong arm, dusted off my jacket with the back of his hand, and asked, "Will ye not come aboard the *Covenant* and see the full scope of a sailing ship?"

I looked, too, at the seamen in the skiff at the wharf. . . .

It was then that I saw my uncle standing by. He said, "Come aboard the brig for a half an hour, lad."

Now, I was not going to put myself in jeopardy, so I told the captain that my uncle and I had an appointment with a lawyer.

"Ay," the captain said. "The boat will set ye ashore at the town pier, and that's but a penny stonecast from Rankeillor's house." And here he suddenly leaned over and whispered in my ear, "Be careful of the old fox, Ebenezer. He means mischief. Come aboard till I can get a word with ye." And then, passing his arm through mine, he continued aloud, as he set off toward his boat, "Come see the many treasures we have from the Americas: Indian feather-work, the skin of a wild beast, a mockingbird that meows like a cat, a cardinal bird that is as red as blood. Whichever one ye may want, ye may have."

By this time we were boat-side at the wharf, and we climbed into a skiff, and headed for the *Covenant*. I thought I had found a good friend in Captain Hoseason, and I now was very happy to see the ship.

When we were alongside the *Covenant*, Hoseason helped me aboard first. On deck, he instantly slipped his arm back under mine. There I stood awhile, a little dizzy with the unsteadiness of the rocking of the ship and the busyness of the crew, yet vastly pleased with these strange sights.

"But where is my uncle?" I asked, finally coming to my senses.

"Ay," said Hoseason, with a sudden grimness, "that's the point."

A gripping fear came over me. With all my strength, I plucked myself clear of him and ran to the side of the ship. Sure enough, there was the skiff being rowed quickly toward the town, with my uncle sitting in the stern. I gave a piercing cry—"Help, help!"—but my uncle only turned round and showed me a face full of cruelty and greed.

Then strong hands grabbed me back from the ship's side, and a thunderbolt seemed to strike over me. I saw a great flash and fell senseless.

CHAPTER FOUR

I came to in darkness, in great pain, bound hand and foot, and deafened by many unfamiliar sounds: the roaring of water, the thundering of the sails, and the shrill cries of seamen. I was so sick and hurt that it took me a long while to realize that I must be lying somewhere in the belly of the ship.

And so it was, I was kidnapped! A prisoner of my uncle's doings! When my head stopped throbbing, I thought through my plight and assumed I was being taken from Scotland. And with no measure of time, day and night were alike to me in that ill-smelling cavern. How long I lay there, I do not know.

At long last I was startled fully awake with the blast of a firearm on deck and then surprised by the light of a hand-lantern shining in my face. Someone grabbed me and dragged me up on deck. It took several minutes for my eyes to adjust to the glare off the ocean.

Captain Hoseason approached me and said, "We need a new cabin boy. Will you work in our roundhouse?"

"Where are you taking me?" I demanded to know.

"The Carolinas," he replied coolly. "You'll fetch a fine price to work in the tobacco fields."

"As a slave?" My mind reeled. I looked desperately at the ocean below me and saw the body of what must have been the prior cabin boy bobbing face-down in the water. The expanse of red that spread out around him told me he had been the victim of the gunshot I heard belowdecks! I stared and stared, realizing that it was not in my interest to disagree with these men.

So I nodded my head in consent—I would be their cabin boy for the voyage. For the next few days, I served the men their usual meal of porridge and every so often a dram of liquor, if the captain gave the word. The round-house, where the seamen ate, stood some six feet above the decks and was of good dimensions. It was fitted from top to bottom with lockers for the officers' belongings.

A small window with a shutter on each side, and a skylight in the roof, gave it light by day, and it was from here that I watched the shore when I could. We were going north around Scotland, and were now on the high sea between the Orkney and Shetland Islands.

It was on the tenth day of our voyage as I reckoned when a great fog settled over the ship as thick as a cloud. Just as I sat at the roundhouse window, wondering how we could possibly sail in such a state, I heard a great crash near the front of the *Covenant.* I dashed to the deck and found some of the men hanging over the side, listening as the sound of splintered wood came up from the water. At first I thought our ship had run aground and was punctured. But then the truth dawned on me: We had struck a smaller ship—probably split her, from the sound of it. There was a brief yell or two, but we could see nothing for the fog. Soon the cries came from behind us, and then stopped.

"There'll be no survivors," said the captain.

I was appalled at the captain's coldheartedness. People were calling for help! I wanted to shout out that we should halt the ship to look for anybody left alive when, all of a sudden, a voice came from over our bowsprit at the front of the vessel.

"Avast, there," called a man's voice. "Will no one help me?"

We rushed to the bow to see a man clinging for his life. What luck and agility! I thought as he was pulled onto the deck. He must have leapt onto our bowsprit just as the ships met. He was brought to the roundhouse and I fetched him a dram of whiskey.

I dashed to the deck and found some of the men hanging over the side, listening as the sound of splintered wood came up from the water.

He was smallish in stature and his face was heavily freckled from the sun. His eyes had a kind of dancing madness in them that was both engaging and alarming, and when he unbuttoned his greatcoat, he laid a pair of fine silver-mounted pistols on the table. I saw that he also wore a great sword as well as a money belt that was bulging with coinage.

Captain Hoseason looked him up and down, seemingly genuinely impressed with his dandy attire and the fine silver buttons upon his coat. "Ye've a French soldier's coat upon your back and a Scotch tongue in your head," he said. "Most peculiar."

"Ay," said the gentleman.

"I have known many a Jacobite who have hidden from the British army near these parts, before they sail to France," the captain said in a probing manner.

"Would it be against your politics to have a Jacobite on board?" the man asked coyly.

"I care little for politics," the captain exclaimed. "Only money. And if the Devil offered me sterling, then I would sail him around the Horn of Africa."

"Well, then," said the man, "I am a Jacobite man. If I am found by King George's redcoats, it will be the end of Alan Breck of the Stewart clan." By this I understood him to mean himself.

I had never seen a Jacobite before and did not know quite what to make of him yet.

He continued, "I was returning to France before your ship split our vessel. If ye can set me ashore where I was going, I will reward ye for your trouble."

"In France?" said the captain. "No, sir, that I cannot do. But let me ask you, how much is it worth to you not to be found?"

"Thirty guineas," returned Alan Breck very quickly, "if you drop me off at the seaside along your route, or sixty if ye set me on the Linnhe Loch."

The captain's eyes narrowed. "And what if I take the whole belt?"

Despite the rocking of the boat, Alan Breck leapt nimbly to his feet and put his hand upon his cutlass handle. "Take it from me and ye will not see nightfall."

I thought this man to be rather brash, what with a captain of a crew of murderers and slave traders on board. And yet, at once I respected his courage. He struck me as an honest man, and honesty was a rare trait upon the *Covenant*.

The captain saw the steel in the Jacobite's eyes. "Sixty guineas it is," he said, softening. "I am going to my cabin now, and when I return we'll share a drink over the agreement. Bring him some dinner," he said to me. And with that he left the roundhouse with his men following.

"And so you are a Jacobite?" I asked as I set meat before Alan Breck.

"Ay," he said as he sat down and began to eat. "And from the looks of the clothes ye wear, ye are no doubt from the lowlands."

"Yes, from Essendean," I replied. But I well knew why he mentioned the fact that I looked like I was from the lowlands. Lowland folk were more apt to be loyal to the King of England, not Bonnie Prince Charlie, the man the Jacobites considered to be the true king. "I believe that George II is the true king of England and Scotland," I told him, seeing no need to repay his honesty with anything but the truth. "But I harbor no ill will to those who would rather see Prince Charlie of the Stewart clan on the throne."

Alan Breck paused a moment to stare at me before he continued. "What is yer name, lad?" he asked between bites of food.

"David Balfour."

"Well, David Balfour. Ye have neither the rough-and-tumble manner nor the look of any other member of this crew as I have seen so far. Are ye a runaway?"

"Nay, stolen. I was kidnapped to be sold as a slave in the Carolinas."

"Then ye'll not be adverse to telling me what kind of men the captain and his crew are."

"Murderers," I replied bluntly. I paused to allow him to reflect upon my answer. "You will not leave this ship alive if you trust them."

"Ay," he agreed. "That is the feeling I have. These knaves are as treacherous as the Red Fox."

The Red Fox! I thought. Even a lowland lad such as myself had heard of the scourge of the Highland clans, Colin Roy Campbell, or the Red Fox as he was known. It was the Red Fox who enforced the king's orders to disarm all of Bonnie Prince Charlie's supporters of their weapons of war: swords, pikes, battle-axes, and even bagpipes. From the way Alan Breck said the name "Red Fox," I knew he despised him as a pastor does sin.

"Have you ever come up against him?" I asked, my curiosity getting the better of me.

"Nay, lad," he replied, his tone heavy and serious. "But if I did, there is nay doubt that he would not live long after that."

Was this Alan Breck a killer of British soldiers? I thought. Would he take my life because I was not a Jacobite? I believe he intentionally brought up the topic of the Red Fox to test my reaction, despite what I told him previously as to my feelings about Jacobites. I said nothing and did not change my expression.

"Ye're a cool one," he said, breaking into a smile. "I can trust ye, no doubt."

Then, from belowdecks, we heard the clang of cutlasses being handed out.

"The captain, I'm guessing, is right now planning my death. Will ye fight with a Jacobite?"

"I'll stand with you," I assured him.

He leapt up and watched his plate slide off the table to the floor. The ocean was growing fiercer, rocking the *Covenant* wildly.

"Good!" he shouted. "If we survive this ordeal, ye shall be repaid hand-somely." With that, he ripped a silver button from his sleeve and handed it to me. Upon it was a family crest which I assumed was the Stewart clan's.

"This is only a down payment," he continued. "And if ye find yourself stranded in the Highlands, show that button, and ye'll be welcome in any freedom-loving Jacobite home."

I pocketed it and nodded. He then handed me his two pistols, a powder horn, and a small bag of bullets that had been tied to his belt.

"Ye shall protect my rear." By this he meant the window and the skylight. "I shall face the door," he continued. "For it is from there that the main force will attack." Thereupon he drew his great sword and made a slash with it through the air, testing the width of the room.

The tramp of feet and shouting of the crew drew closer to the roundhouse door, and then above us.

"How many will be against us?" Alan asked quickly.

I made a quick tally of the crew in my mind. "Fifteen," I said with a dry mouth. Whether it was from the lurching of the ship or the thought of the coming confrontation, my chest was tight and my knees were growing weaker by the moment.

"Show neither fear nor mercy!" Alan shouted, steeling his own courage.

He quickly drew out his dirk, which he held tightly in his left hand. Positioning himself in front of the door, Alan flexed at the knees enough to take into account the increasing rocking of the ship. I clambered up into the berth with the pistols and opened the window where I was to watch. The wind dove into the room, blasting me in the face with a gush of coldness. Night was falling, and the fog had been blown away by the shrieking wind.

My heart beat like a bird's, both quick and little, when I heard over the booming of the ocean a dozen pair of feet coming through the ship for us. As for hope, I had none. I looked at Alan, and he at me. We understood each other in that brief glance: This was a fight to the death.

Then the crew was upon us!

"Steady on, lad!" Alan roared. I heard the terrible clang of metal upon metal. Over my shoulder I saw Alan dodge and then run a man through with his blade.

Just then one of the crew tried to come in through the window. I had never fired a pistol in my life, but it was now or never. And just as he swung his leg over the sash, I cried out "Take that!" and pulled the trigger.

My attacker screamed and fell backward, but another one took his place. I fired with the second pistol and watched as this sailor also reeled back, grabbing his chest. Then I looked around—the roundhouse was filling with the smoke of my shots. And though the ship lurched violently in the turbulent ocean, there was Alan, standing as before, with his sword running blood to the hilt.

Swelled with triumph, and looking invincible, Alan turned to me and shouted, "Recharge your pistols! They'll come through the skylight next."

And sure as the world, the glass of the skylight was dashed into a thousand pieces, and a man leaped through and landed on the floor. I grabbed at my ammunition to reload, but, to my horror, I spilled the bag of bullets. As the ship rocked, every last one ran off the table and onto the floor.

The man drew his dirk from his belt. I backed away from him and grabbed at the wall. Just as my hand found the handle of a cutlass, the ship lurched again. The intruder grabbed my shoulder for balance, but only succeeded in toppling us both over.

As the crest of a wave crashed through the open window, I scrambled to be rid of my attacker. But the ship was listing badly, and instead of finding the floor, I was climbing the tilting wall. As I reached for the window and clawed at its pane, a hand grabbed me from below. I kicked at it violently.

The ship suddenly righted itself, and I found myself more out the window than in it. And through the haze of the gun smoke, I saw the determined Alan

Over my shoulder I saw Alan dodge and then run a man through with his blade.

Breck Stewart fighting for his life as Hoseason's crew led another assault through the door. The sword in his hand flashed like quicksilver into the huddle of our enemies, and at every flash there came the scream of a man wounded.

This was my last image of the inside of the *Covenant*, for as I tried to make my way back into the roundhouse, a tremendous crash came from belowdecks. With a mighty jolt, the ship seemed to shake me off its side, and I plunged back-first into the stinging cold ocean.

I clawed at the surface of the sea until I felt something solid.

CHAPTER FIVE

I rose up from the depths of the ocean kicking and screaming, desperate for air. It is said that a man who goes under for the third time goes down for good, but I was three times that number and the power to fight for a breath had still not left me. I clawed at the surface of the sea until I felt something solid.

It was a spare yard that I had got hold of. I yelled to the ship, but I was too far off to be heard above the roar of the ocean. The ship was being battered badly by the wind and surf, and it seemed everyone was too busy fighting to tend to it. Then the mainmast splintered and separated from the ship with a shuddering snap.

I thought of Alan momentarily, hoping he had escaped, but my own survival was pressing at my attention. Spying an outcropping of land, I grasped the yard with both arms, kicked with my feet, and headed toward it.

I was at the last of my energy when I finally stumbled upon shore. I looked about in the moonlight to see a desolate and deserted landscape. But it was dry land, and I was safe.

At the first light of morning, I saw that the fog had again descended upon both land and sea. I put on my shoes and climbed a rugged hill of big blocks of granite. When I reached the top, I scanned the sea, but there was no sign of the ship. I was afraid to think what had befallen Alan.

In addition to my wet clothes and weariness, my belly began to ache with hunger. So I set off eastward along the south coast, hoping to find a house where I might warm myself. I walked and walked but found little except a jumble of granite rocks with heather in among them and a creek running into the sea. Exhausted, I drifted off into slumber by a rock that partially hid me from the rain.

I must have slept some time, for when I awoke the sun fell upon me. The fog had blown away, and I looked to see that my island lay only several hundred

I walked and walked but found little . . .

yards off the coast. And, joy!, a small town stood upon the mainland. This raised my spirits and sullened my heart in the same moment. Here before me was, no doubt, a warm fire, a meal, and other people. But how to get across?

Had I been a sea-bred boy, the solution might have already presented itself. But I was country born and more akin to fields than the sea. As I pondered my situation and the sun grew warmer and the air sweeter, I noticed that the sea appeared to be going out, departing the shores of my isle. As it pulled back it left a path of sand, which I later learned was called a jetty.

I sprang into the surf and half waded, half walked my way toward the village. At any moment I expected the tide to surge back and drown me like the Pharaoh's army chasing after Moses, but the farther I walked, the easier it became, until finally I scampered upon dry land.

The first house I came upon was in the bottom of a hollow. It was low and longish, roofed with turf and on a mound in front of it sat an old gentleman smoking his pipe in the sun. He let me know that I was in the Ross of Mull, and that through the night, he said, several waterlogged men had passed by that very house.

"Was there one," I asked, "dressed like a gentleman?"

"Ay," he replied. "One wore breeches and stockings, while the rest had sailors' trousers."

"Alan is safe!" I cried with relief. And then the old gentleman clapped his hand to his brow and cried out that I must be the lad with the silver button.

"Why, yes!" I said excitedly.

"Well, then," he said, "I have a word for you. Because he was the only man dressed proper, I opened the door for him. But he would not stop and partake of any food. He merely gave me instructions to pass on to a lad who had his silver button. You are to follow your friend to the town of Torosay." With that he invited me into his house where his wife fed me oat-bread and a cold grouse. The food sat well in my stomach, and I thanked my host and set out upon the road.

Along my journey I passed many Highland folk. Their manner was very agreeable although their dress was strange to see. The Red Fox had issued a law against their wearing their traditional tartan kilt, to punish them for their rebellion. Since then, these folk had taken to wearing short pants, and even only a greatcoat which hung down to their knees.

I knew Torosay to be my destination and repeated the name again and again for directions. But I could tell that the country folk did not entirely trust me because of my lowland accent and proper attire. Thinking at long last that I was lost, I decided to offer two shillings to the next man I met to lead me to Torosay.

I soon overtook a great, ragged man moving quickly but feeling before him with a staff. He was quite blind. I shook my head and laughed at the decision I recently made in regards to paying for a guide.

"Are ye lost?" he asked, hearing me.

"Yes," I replied, astonished at his perceptiveness.

"I can tell by the shuffling of your feet," he continued. "Ye'll be needing someone to walk ye through the Highlands."

I said that I did not see how a blind man could be a guide; but at that he laughed aloud, and said his stick was eyes enough for an eagle.

"See now," he said, striking left and right with his staff, "down there is a running creek, and at the bend of it there stands a bit of a small hill with a stone cocked upon the top of it. And that points the way to Torosay. I know every stone and heather-bush here in Mull."

He was right in every feature, so I told him of my amazement.

"Ha!" he said, "that's nothing. If I had my pistol with me, I could shoot an agent of the Red Fox not twenty paces off, on the other side of the creek."

"Aren't weapons outlawed in the Highlands?" I asked, though I could plain see the butt of a pistol peaking out from the front of his waistcoat.

At this his voice grew thick with suspicion. "Ye sound to me like ye are not from these parts. Are ye a British spy? Do ye work for the Red Fox?"

I quickly assured him that I did not work for the Red Fox, know him, or even know what he looked like. But, with that suspicion lodged in his mind, he never again did warm to me. In fact, his tone grew harsher as we went along.

When we reached a hill that overlooked Torosay, I reached into my pocket for the two shillings I had promised him. The blind man must have thought I was reaching for a weapon, because he reached for his pistol with the speed of a lad twenty years his junior.

But I, being nearly thirty years his junior, was quicker. I knocked his hand away and drew out the weapon, cocked it, and aimed it at him.

"I know not the reason for your animosity against me," I stated flatly. "There is Torosay ahead. Hold out your hand and you shall have your two shillings." He did and I paid him. "As for your weapon . . . ," I began, dislodging the flint from the firing mechanism. I lifted the pistol to my mouth and spit into the firing pan, rendering it useless.

"Here is undoubtedly your only friend back," I said with a touch of sarcasm, handing him back his pistol and flint. "Now be off." He snatched it with a sneer, turned on his heel, and began tapping his stick down the road.

He did not get more than fifty paces away before he turned my way and shouted, "Ye'll find nothing but death in the Highlands, ye blackguard, and I hope it finds ye soon!" With that he disappeared into the dale.

The town of Torosay was small with only one inn to provide lodging to travelers. I secured a room, but before putting to bed, I quietly asked the innkeeper about Alan Breck. He told me that I should talk to a man named Neil Roy Stewart, who operated a ferry to Morven. Since Stewart was the name of Alan Breck's clan, I reasoned that this Neil Roy would know where Alan was.

I resolved that at first light I would seek out Neil Roy Stewart.

At this his voice grew thick with suspicion.

Chapter Six

*I*n the morning I found Neil Roy Stewart at the town's dock. By way of introduction I showed him the silver button Alan had given to me.

"Put that away, lad," he said. "It is not safe to shine that about even in these parts. I know Alan Breck. He is a fair heather-cat, appearing and disappearing when he likes. He passed this way only yesterday morning. He intends to get a ship to France, and I intend to join him." He paused for a moment, then added, "He instructed me to tell you to make your way to his home in Aucharn. You are only a day's journey behind him. It is not an easy road there, but you will be safe."

Neil Roy then invited me to sail with him to Morven upon his ferry. From there I could make my way to Aucharn. The journey from Torosay proved slow due to slight winds. But it did give me ample time to talk to Neil Roy.

The advice he gave me was this: "Speak to no one by the way, and leave the road and lie in the heather if you see any redcoats coming your way. In short, conduct yourself like a robber or a Jacobite."

I parted ways with Neil Roy at Morven seaside, and quickly set out. The road to Aucharn was a long one but uneventful, save for the moving clump of scarlet I saw along the waterside as a ferry carried me across Loch Leven.

"What is that?" I asked the captain of the ship.

"Redcoats," he replied, setting me onshore. "Be careful, be safe, and keep yer distance from those British soldiers."

I sat down to eat some oat-bread that I had saved from breakfast and thought about my situation. Here I was in a strange land, going to join up with an outlaw. If I had used my sense, I probably would have struck off immediately back to my lowland home. But as I was sitting and thinking, the sound of men and horses came to me through the wood. Presently four travelers came into view.

The first was a great, redheaded gentleman. The second, by his decent black garb and white wig, I took to be a lawyer. The third was a servant, walking alongside, leading his horse by its reins. As for the fourth, who brought up the tail, I had seen his like before, and knew him at once to be a sheriff's officer.

Perhaps it was the food in my stomach that gave me some bravery, for I rose up and asked the first man the way to Aucharn.

"What business do you have hiding by the road like a thieving highwayman?" the lawyer asked. And then turning to the redheaded fellow, he warned, "Careful, Colin Roy, many a Jacobite are traveling this route to Aucharn."

"My loyalty is to our King George," I objected. "I am a Balfour of the House of Shaws, originally from Essendean."

"And I am a Campbell of Glenure," the redheaded gentleman said haughtily, peering down from his steed. "I have the king's business to be about. So tell me quickly, why are you on this road?"

I could not answer. I stood as if struck dumb. Colin Roy Campbell of Glenure—it couldn't be true. Colin Roy Campbell . . . the Red Fox!

But the shock of this discovery was small compared to the next one. For at that moment, a shot rang out from higher up the hill, and Colin Roy fell from his horse. A covey of pheasants sprang into flight from their hiding in the heather, and the horses neighed and stomped their hooves. The whole road seemed to have awoken instantly from the shot. And then, just as quickly, near silence returned. The birds were gone and the horses calmed themselves. I moved closer to the prostrate body of the Red Fox, as did the other men.

He gasped for breath several times before he began to spit up blood.

"Take care of yourselves," Colin Roy said in a soft, sad voice. "I am dead." He tried to open his clothes as if to look for a wound, but his fingers slipped on the buttons. With that he gave a great sigh, his head rolled on his shoulder, and he breathed no more.

The lawyer didn't say a word, but the servant broke out into a great noise of crying and weeping. I stared at the whole deathly scene with a kind of horror. The sheriff's officer had run for help at the first sound of the shot. I watched him come around the turn with a troop of redcoats close on his heels.

It was the sight of that scarlet horde that brought me to my senses. I scrambled up the hill, away from the ghastly murder. Then I caught sight of the back of a man near the woods. He was a big man in a black coat and carried a long fowling piece.

"The murderer! The murderer!" I cried out. "Here! I see him!"

The man glanced over his shoulder and began to run. In a moment he disappeared into a fringe of birches, and I saw him no more. I ran after him until someone from the road shouted to me to stop. I halted and looked back.

The lawyer and the sheriff's officer were standing at the bottom of the hill, just above the road, waving to me to come back. To their left, the redcoats, muskets in hand, were already climbing the hill.

"He's up there," I cried out. "Follow me!"

But instead, the lawyer shouted, "Ten pounds if you take that lad! He's an accomplice. He was posted here to hold us in talk."

My heart leapt into my mouth with quite a new kind of terror. They thought I was part of the plot!

"In here!" a familiar voice whispered urgently from the trees. I scarcely knew what I was doing, but I obeyed it to be out of the sights of the redcoats' muskets. As I did so I heard firelocks bang and saw the balls strike and splinter the birches around me.

Just inside the shelter of the trees I found Alan Breck Stewart. "Come!" he cried, and set off running along the side of the mountain; and I, like a sheep, followed him.

He was a big man in a black coat and carried a long fowling piece.

CHAPTER SEVEN

*A*lan Breck and I raced through the birches away from the redcoats, sometimes creeping behind low humps on the mountainside, sometimes crawling on all fours among the heather. The pace was deadly.

Just as my heart was bursting against my ribs, Alan stopped. We threw ourselves down in a small patch of woods. He lay there with his face in the leaves, panting like a dog.

After we lay there for who knows how long, Alan came round. He went to the border of the woods, peered out, and then returned and sat down.

"Well," he said, raising an eyebrow and smiling mischievously, "that was some excitement, Davie."

I said nothing. I had seen murder done, a gentleman struck out of life in a moment, and the pity of that sight was still sore within me. Murder was done upon the man Alan hated; here was Alan skulking in the trees and running from the troops, and whether his was the hand that fired, or only ordered it, meant little to me. I held him in horror and could scarcely look upon his face.

"Are ye still tired?" he asked.

"No," I said. "No, but you and I must part. I like you very much, Alan, but your ways are not mine, and they are not God's."

Alan's eyes grew wide, and taking out his dirk and laying his hand upon it, he said, "I swear upon the Holy Iron that I had no part in that deed."

"Upon your honor," I cried, sitting up, "you had no hand in it at all?"

"As one friend to another," Alan said with much seriousness, "if I were going to kill a gentleman, it would not be in my own country. That would only bring trouble upon my clan. These hills are full of Jacobites who despise the Red Fox, David. Any red-blooded Highlander could have done the deed without me. And do you think I would do without a gun or sword to defend myself? Do you think I'm a fool?"

"Well," I said after a moment's pause, "that's true. You are no fool, from what I have witnessed." I offered him my hand.

We shook hands as gentlemen do after a cross word between them.

"Now let's take a peek at the redcoats," Alan said. Looking out between the fringe of trees, we could see an exceedingly steep side of a mountain running down into the waters of the lake. It was a rough face, all hanging stone and heather, and big clumps of birches. And away at the far end toward a town Alan said was Balachulish, little red soldiers were dipping up and down over hill and dale, growing smaller every minute.

Alan smiled to himself. "We would not be safe going to Aucharn, Davie. The redcoats will look there first for me. We'll strike out for Cluny's Cage."

I started to ask what Cluny's Cage was, but before I could speak, Alan was already plunging deep into the heather.

The road to Cluny's Cage was oftentimes treacherous, and more than once Alan's steady hand kept me from slipping on moss-covered rocks. We were always mindful of redcoats as well, and hid in the heather and the hills to avoid being spotted.

When the shadow of night fell, we would set forth with more boldness, standing our full height and stepping out at a good pace.

After a few days, Alan was pleased enough with our progress to begin whistling a number of Highland airs, confident that no redcoat was near enough to hear. Little did we know that we were being watched.

Day began with the moorfowl crying in the heather, and the light coming slowly clearer in the east. Like blind men we stumbled down a heathery brae when the heather gave a rustle and three or four ragged men leaped out. In a moment we were lying on our backs, each with a dirk at his throat.

CHAPTER EIGHT

*T*looked up into the face of the man who held a knife to my throat. Due either to my exhaustion or my trust in Alan, I was not afraid of him. Then I heard Alan whisper something in Gaelic and the dirks were put away. The men left us without a word.

"They are Cluny's men," Alan told me. "Cluny Macpherson, the chief of the clan Vourich," he explained, "had been one of the leaders of the great rebellion six years ago. There is a price on his head, so his men are a bit protective."

"So Cluny is still here?" I asked, remembering that Alan had earlier mentioned the term "Cluny's Cage" to me. I was intrigued.

"Ay, still in his own country and still among his old clan. King George would love to stretch his neck, but he'll never find him." And saying nothing more, Alan rolled on his face in a deep heather-bush, and seemed to sleep at once.

So we lay there, Alan sleeping, and I imagining what Cluny's Cage must be. A jail? A pen to hold wild animals? Various vague and sometimes sinister thoughts were floating through my mind when the men returned. Cluny would be glad to receive us, we were told. So, journeying through a labyrinth of dreary glens and hollows, we came to the foot of a steep woods, which scrambled up a craggy hillside and was crowned by a naked precipice.

"It's there," said one of the guides, and we struck up the hill. The trees clung upon the slope like sailors on the shrouds of a ship, and their trunks were like the rungs of a ladder which we grabbed and climbed.

When we reached our destination, we could scarce make out what it was, so well was it disguised. A tree, which grew out from the hillside, was the living center-beam of the roof. The walls were twined branches and were covered with moss. The whole house had something of an egg shape, and it half hung,

. . . more than once Alan's steady hand kept me from slipping on moss-covered rocks.

half stood in that steep, hillside thicket like a wasp's nest in a green hawthorn shrub. So this was Cluny's Cage.

It was large enough to shelter five or six people with some comfort. A projection of the cliff had been cleverly cut for the fireplace, and the rising smoke escaped notice because it was similar in color to the rocks. It was the perfect place to hide.

When we came to the door, Cluny was seated by his rock chimney. Though dressed plainly with an old knitted nightcap drawn over his ears, he had the manners of a king. It was quite a sight to see him rise out of his place to welcome us.

"Step in, gentlemen," Cluny said in a friendly manner. "I welcome ye to my house." We went inside, and the men raised the customary dram of Scotch whiskey for the death of King George. I refused a drink, complaining about my weak stomach, but it was really that I did not wish the king any harm. Then Alan explained to me why Cluny lived like a lonely mole in the side of a cliff. Though stripped of all legal power by an act of Parliament, he still exercised a patriarchal justice in his clan. Disputes were brought to him by the men of his country who laid aside revenge and paid down money at his mere word.

On that first day, Cluny prepared a meal of venison for us, giving it as much attention and care as an old maid would have. When eating was through, he then brought out an overly thumbed, greasy pack of cards. I instantly remembered my father's words from my youth telling me that gambling was no way for a man to get ahead in the world. I excused myself and left the men at the table.

What with the journey and the venison, a strange heaviness soon came over me, and I had scarce laid down upon the bed before I fell into a kind of trance in which I continued almost the whole time of our stay in the Cage. Sometimes I was wide awake and understood what passed, and sometimes I only heard voices. I realized I was ill from the exposure to the cold and heat, the crouching in the wet heather for hours at a time, and eating little. From my few waking episodes, I saw that Alan and Cluny spent most of their time at cards.

On the second day, at about noon, Alan came over to my bed and put his face close to mine. Cluny sat at his table, holding the pack of cards.

Alan asked me for a loan of money.

"What for?" I asked, still groggy from sleep.

"Oh, just for a loan," he said.

"But why? I don't see why."

"Davie," Alan said tenderly, "ye wouldn't grudge me a loan?"

I would, though, if I had had my senses! But all I thought of then was to get his face away, and I handed him my money.

On the morning of the third day I awoke with a great relief of spirits. I had a mind to eat and rose from my bed. It was a gray day with a cool, mild air. I saw the cards on the table, but no gold, only a heap of little written papers, and these on Cluny's side. Alan had an odd, troubled look about him.

"David," he said at last, "I've lost our money. That's the naked truth."

"My money too?" I asked.

"Your money too," he replied, standing his ground.

I couldn't believe what I heard. It was as though I was still asleep and dreaming. What little money I had saved from my youth and the small amount Mr. Campbell of Essendean had given me was gone. My fists curled up and my face grew red. Here I was in a strange countryside with nary a halfpenny and no hope for making any. And I was ashamed, too, because I felt I had been tricked like some country Johnny. I had not the heart to ask Cluny for my money back. Instead, I took out my anger on Alan by ignoring all his entreaties to talk to me. I stewed in my fury and said not a word to Alan Breck.

CHAPTER NINE

When I was feeling somewhat better, we were able to continue on our way. Rumors had reached the cage that Alan was somehow responsible for the Red Fox's death. And though Alan again claimed his innocence, Cluny did not think it safe for us to remain there. Alan agreed. And though I was still sore at him for his behavior with my money, I knew that Alan alone could safely lead us out of the Highlands. We set off at dawn with some oatmeal, dried venison, two pistols for Alan to replace the ones he had lost on board the *Covenant,* and a sword for me.

We were ferried across Loch Errocht under the cover of fog and went down its eastern shore to another hiding place near the head of Loch Rannoch. Alan and I had said nothing since we left Cluny's Cage, had simply marched along in silence: I, angry and proud, and Alan ashamed that he had lost my money as well as upset that I should take it so hard.

After crossing Loch Rannoch, we went round the valleys of Glen Lyon, Glen Lochay, and Glen Dochart and came down upon the lowlands by Kippen and the upper waters of the Forth.

This next week of our journey was a dreadful time, rendered worse by the gloom of the weather and the country. I was never warm; my teeth chattered in my head, I was troubled with a very sore throat, and I had a stitch in my side that never left me. All the while I slept in a wet bed with rain beating above and mud oozing below me. The sickness that I thought I had left behind at Cluny's Cage revisited me. I was miserable.

For the better part of two days, Alan was unusually kind: silent, but always ready to help. For the same length of time I said nothing, nursing my anger over my lost money, roughly refusing his help and passing over him as if he had been a bush or a stone.

. . . I saw that Alan and Cluny spent most of their time at cards.

The second night, or rather, the peep of the third day, found us upon a very open hill, so that we could not follow our usual plan to lie down immediately and sleep. Before we had reached a place of shelter, the gray had cleared, for though it still rained, the clouds ran higher and swifter. Alan, looking into my face, showed some concern, for I felt as worn out as an old shoe, and I'm sure it showed.

"Ye had better let me take your pack," he said.

"I do very well, thank you," I replied, cold as ice.

Alan's temper flashed. "I'll not offer it again. I'm not a patient man."

"I never said you were," I said, sounding like a silly ten-year-old boy. "I am as ready as yourself."

"Ready?" he asked.

"I'm no boaster like some that I could name. Come on!" And in my weariness I gave way to my fury. I drew my sword and pointed it at Alan.

"David!" he cried. "Are ye daft? I can not draw upon ye. It would be murder."

"Then you can add murder to thieving on your list of sins, Alan Breck," I challenged him.

His eyes narrowed and he drew his sword. But before I could touch my blade to his, he let his sword fall to the ground. "Nay, nay—I can't. I can't," he said.

At this, the last of my anger oozed all out of me, and I found myself sick, sorry, and wondering what I had been thinking. I would have given the world to take back what I had said, but a word once spoken can never be recaptured. I remembered all of Alan's kindness and courage in the past, and how he had helped and cheered me in our difficult days. He had been father and brother and friend to me. And never did I have a better or more caring companion.

"Alan," I croaked, "I am not mad at you. I did not appreciate your losing all the money I had in the world, but you did not intend it. Every time I think of having my money taken from me, I see my uncle's face." And for the first time, I told him in detail of my uncle's treachery.

Alan listened with increasing fury. When I was through, he shouted, "Ay! Something will have to be done about that!"

At that moment the sickness that hung upon me seemed to double, and the pang in my side felt like the tip of a sword. I dropped to my knees.

At long last, I put my pride away. "Alan, if you can't help me, I think I will die here."

"Can ye walk?" he asked.

"No," I answered, "not without help. This last hour my legs have been fainting under me."

"Let me get my arms around ye so I can lift ye." Which he did. "Now lean hard upon me," he ordered. Alan came near to sobbing as we started to walk. "Davie, I have neither sense nor kindness. I did not remember that you were still a lad."

"Let's say no more about it," I said, stopping his apology.

"Right ye are. We're in Balquidder, and there should be plenty of friends' houses where we can stop and get ye patched up. But we can't continue to run and hide like this forever. When ye are again well enough to travel, we'll set out for Queensferry and your lawyer friend. For I feel that all this hiding in the heather will be the very death of ye."

CHAPTER TEN

*A*t the door of the first house we came to, Alan knocked and was kindly welcomed by an old acquaintance of his, Duncan Dhu. I was put to bed without delay, and soon a doctor was fetched. He found me in sorry shape. It wasn't until a month had passed that I was able to take the road again with a good heart. All that time Alan would not leave me. He hid by day in a nearby wood; and at night, when the coast was clear, he would come into the house to visit me.

This time of my recovery was joyous. Duncan Dhu had a set of bagpipes and he commonly turned night into day with their merry sound. First Duncan would blow, then Alan, and then any Jacobite who passed through the house hiding from the redcoats. All night long the pipes changed hands, and I dare say it picked up the spirits of this lowland lad to hear them played in such a festive manner.

August arrived with beautiful, warm weather, and by the time the middle of the month was upon us, I was pronounced fit to travel by the doctor. Alan and I decided that we would head straight to Queensferry. There I could meet with Mr. Rankeillor, and contend with my uncle, and Alan hoped to contact a kin in Edinburgh who would help him find a way to France.

We caught a skiff going across the river Hope before sunrise, and I found myself in Queensferry before the sun rose. We agreed that Alan would lie in the fields outside town until he heard me whistling, just to be safe.

Just being in the town where I had been betrayed was enough to rekindle the fury I felt toward Ebenezer. I resolved that this time I would not be duped or made a fool of by my uncle. I quickly found Mr. Rankeillor's house. He greeted me warmly and welcomed me into his parlor. I sat down and told him my name, what my uncle had done to me, and my adventures.

. . . he commonly turned night into day with their merry sound.

He listened quietly and gravely before he spoke. "I knew your father and your uncle, Ebenezer, when they were young. For your uncle was not always old and bent. Indeed, he once had a fine, handsome air about him.

"Your father and he," Mr. Rankeillor continued, "fell in love with the same lady. After much squabbling they decided that one man would take the lady, the other would take the estate. This was unusual because by custom the elder brother, your father Alexander, would receive the estate. Thus your father and mother lived and died poor while your uncle lived in a grand house, empty and alone. Money was all that Ebenezer got in the bargain, and that is all he has now. No doubt your father never told you this story because he was too proud to admit that he once came from money, but ended up poor."

At this point, Mr. Rankeillor smiled and opened up his hands as though he were offering me a present. "But it matters not what occurred in the past. You are heir to the Shaw estate. No papers exist giving the house to Ebenezer, and since he has no children to put a claim on it, it is yours by right and by custom."

I sat back in a daze. Not only was I to be a proper gentleman, but I would soon have a fortune, and a house as well. Granted, the house was not the magnificent mansion I first imagined, but with some work it could be a grand estate.

"But still, Ebenezer will not give it up willingly," the lawyer interjected, disturbing my reverie, "and certainly not without a fight. I can tell you from experience in these matters that a lawsuit is always expensive, and a family lawsuit is always scandalous. If only there were a way to avoid it . . ." Then he looked at me carefully. "The kidnapping, to be sure, would be in our favor if we could only prove it." And then he paused as though deep in thought.

"As to your friend Alan Breck," Mr. Rankeillor continued, "he is a Highlander, you say? His accent might be the answer! This," he said with a twinkle in his eye, "is what we should do . . . "

I listened, agreed, and left.

I sat down and told him my name. . . .

CHAPTER ELEVEN

*L*ater that night Alan, Mr. Rankeillor, and I made our way to Cramond and the House of Shaws. Mr. Rankeillor and I hid while Alan knocked upon the door. After a minute an upstairs window was thrown open.

"What's this? This is no time of night for decent folk," my uncle croaked. "Mind you, I have a gun."

"Is that you, Mr. Balfour?" returned Alan.

"What brings you here? Who are you?" asked Ebenezer, angrily.

"My name is my own affair," Alan said, "but there is a name you might find of interest."

"And what is it?"

"David," Alan replied.

"What was that?" cried my uncle, in a different voice.

"Shall I give ye the rest of the name, then?" said Alan.

There was a pause; and then, "I'm thinking I'd better let you in," my uncle said, doubtfully.

Ebenezer shut the window, and moments later the front door creaked open.

"And now," he said, "mind that I have a gun."

"Well," Alan said, beginning our story, "my relations found your nephew off the coast of Mull after his ship wrecked. They asked me to give ye a call and confer upon the matter. And I may tell ye, unless we can agree upon some terms, ye are little likely to set eyes upon him again."

My uncle cleared his throat. "I don't care. He wasn't a good lad. I'll pay no ransom for him."

"Well," Alan said in mock surprise, "ye don't want the lad back, is that it? What do ye want done with him, and how much will ye pay?"

"I'm a man of principle," said Ebenezer, simply; "and if I have to pay for it, I'll have to pay for it. And besides, the lad was my brother's son."

"All right, then. Now about the price," Alan said. "What did ye give Captain Hoseason?"

"Hoseason?" cried my uncle, struck aback. "What for?"

"For kidnapping David."

"What do you mean? What did Hoseason tell you?"

"That's my concern."

"Well," my uncle said, clearing his throat. "I gave him twenty pounds to take the boy and sell him in the Carolinas."

"Thank you, Mr. Balfour," Mr. Rankeillor said to Ebenezer, as he and I stepped out from the shadows, "that will do excellently well."

My uncle said not a word, but just sat down on the top doorstep and stared at us like a man turned to stone. Alan took away his gun, plucked him up from the doorstep, and led him into the kitchen. By the time we had the fire lit and a bottle uncorked, my uncle promised Rankeillor to pay me two-thirds of the yearly income of the House of Shaws. Ebenezer would be allowed to live there for as long as I allowed him.

And so I became a man of means and had a name in the country.

In the morning Mr. Rankeillor, Alan, and I set off on the road toward Edinburgh. When we reached the turn to Queensferry, Mr. Rankeillor departed us, assuring me that he would take care of all legal matters pertaining to the House of Shaws. Alan and I continued on our way. We decided that he should keep to the country until a boat could be found to take him back to France. Although the redcoats would not think of looking for him in Edinburgh, he thought it best not to take the chance of being recognized in the city. He gave me instructions to meet with a kinsman of his there who could set up passage for him and any other Highlanders who would join him on a ship to France.

The final leg of the road to Edinburgh was not long and before noon, the same thought—that we were near the time of our parting—was uppermost in both our minds. Like old times, Alan and I walked together in silence till we crested the hill of Corstorphine outside of Edinburgh. Then I insisted he take a large part of the money Mr. Rankeillor had forwarded me from my estate. We both smiled although we were nearer to tears than laughter. And there in front of the Rest-and-be-Thankful Inn we parted.

"Well, good-bye," Alan said, holding out his hand.

"Good-bye, Alan." I grasped his hand and shook it, trying to convey in that brief moment and interaction how much the time we spent together meant to me. Before we met I was but a mere lad, at the whim of men who were to decide my fate. As we left each other, because of his help, I was a man with a fortune and a future. I felt as though somehow I would always be in his debt, and he would always be a friend.

I also had little doubt that he looked upon me with kindness as well, for it is rare for a Highlander to trust and befriend a member outside his clan so readily as Alan did me.

Neither one of us looked the other in the face, nor did I look back at my friend. He would not have wanted it that way. No doubt he was already halfway across the nearest field, striking out for a place to hide, for that was his nature.

My memory of him was bright, and I knew that as the years passed it would never diminish. But the break with Alan was difficult for me. I felt as though I could have sat and wept had not the glorious city of Edinburgh shone before me, inviting me onward, into the busy crowd of life.

Like old times, Alan and I walked together in silence till we crested the hill. . . .

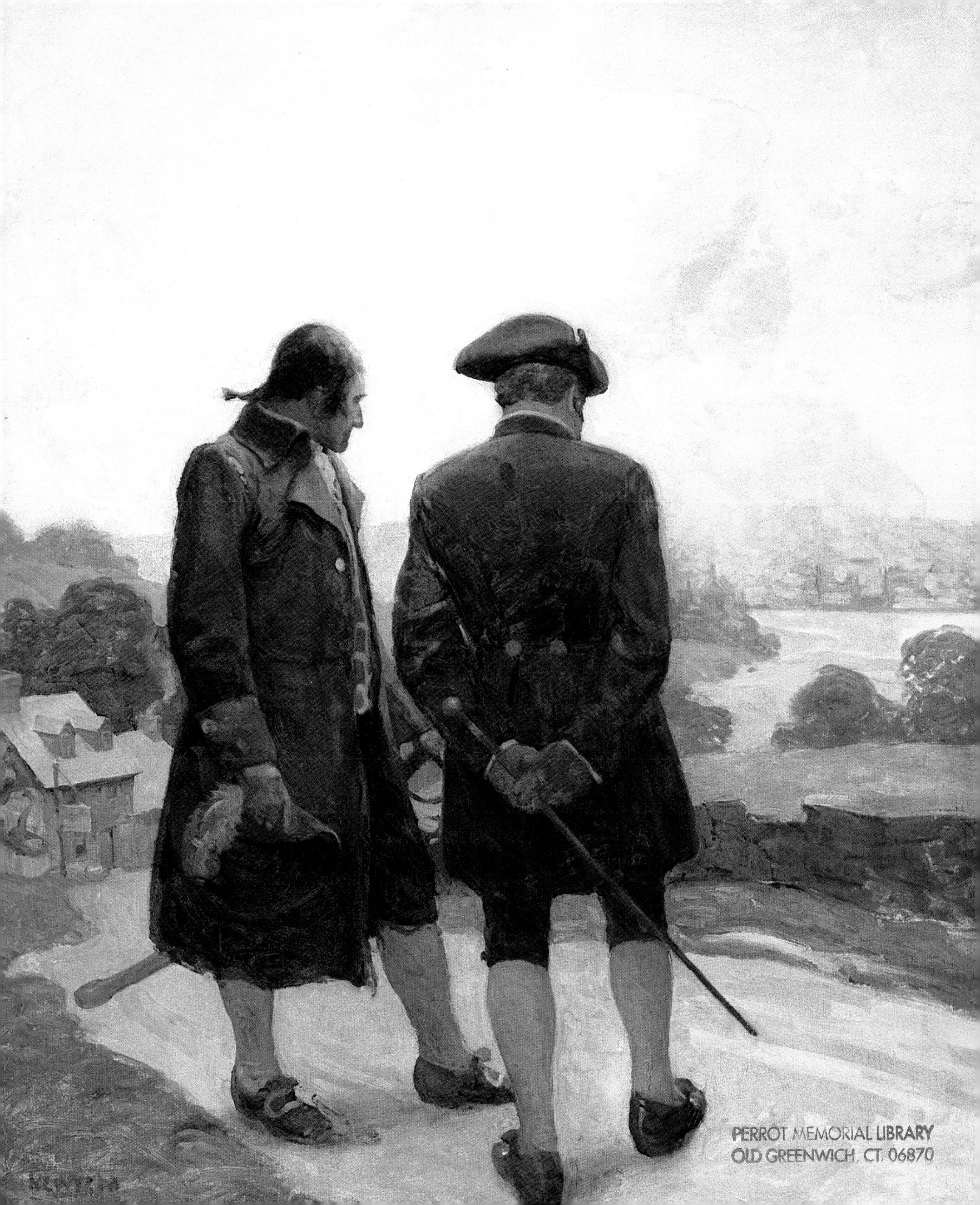

The Covenar